A
Collection of
SHORT STORIES

Dedicated to: My late father, Darrell, my mother Lois, my husband, Ronald, my daughter, Jessica and her family Clay, Christopher, and Aria.

A
Collection of
SHORT STORIES

Rocky T. Kinsley

Order this book online at www.trafford.com
or email orders@trafford.com

Most Trafford titles are also available at major online book retailers.

Printed in the United States of America.

ISBN: 978-1-4269-7130-3 (sc)
ISBN: 978-1-4269-7131-0 (e)

Trafford rev. 07/11/2011

North America & International
toll-free: 1 888 232 4444 (USA & Canada)
phone: 250 383 6864 ♦ fax: 812 355 4082

HER APARTMENT

The clock radio went off at 6:15 AM jerking her to reality. Going to the clean kitchen, she prepared her usual breakfast, a bowl of cereal and a glass of orange juice, always followed by vitamins.

At 6:59 she left her apartment for another day of classes and meetings. Her classes were fifty minutes long that day; she was in one of her depressed moods.

Her classes were over at 11:20. Just enough time for a quick lunch and cigarette before studying in the library. She ate lunch with one her friends who told her about her newest boyfriend. She felt a stab of envy.

By studying from 12:00-3:00, she met all her goals, finish reading Beowulf, study notes from her classes, write two more pages on the critical essay for British Literature, write a short story for Fiction Workshop.

At 3:00 she had a tutoring session with one of her students. The college literary magazine meeting was at 4:30. She gave her opinions on the poems that were submitted.

At 6:00 she took the bus home.

She had supper at 6:30 and then cleaned her clean apartment. She was proud of having a clean home with no family to take care of. At 8:00 the rent had to be paid. As she wrote out the check, she knew that she would watch her money until starting work again in May. As she paid her landlord, he told her to smile; life wasn't that bad. For a few minutes, she chatted with him as they watched his three grandchildren playing in the living room. Again, that familiar stab. With a quick goodnight she returned to her apartment.

Letting Go of the Past

Jean Ann walked out of her English Literature class and down the hall toward her commuter locker. A few more weeks of classes, then finals. After that, she and John would graduate and be married in June. She was looking forward to her career in writing and a life with John. The two had grown up together and had so much in common. Both were intellectual, and loved writing, although in different ways.

"Hey, Jean," called John as she came out the door. She waved and walked through the rain to his car. Although it was raining, she thought that there could never be a more beautiful day. It just seemed too perfect.

"How are things going?" he asked before kissing her.

"Pretty good. How about you?"

They pulled out of the parking lot and started down the street.

"Not too bad. I'm looking forward to graduation though. Hey, I almost forgot to tell you. I got a letter in the mail today from the printing press. I start working as an editor right after we're married."

"Great! I've been looking into some possibilities with some places but nothing definite yet."

"You'll find something. You're a talented writer. Hey, how about a pizza before we go to the library and study?"

"Sure."

"Some of the guys asked me if I could make it to a party Friday night. I told them you and I have plans."

Neither one had ever cared much for the party life on campus. They had friends and were involved in activities on campus, but they never cared for the carefree life that other students led. It had been that way when they were children and all through high school. They had spent all of their time together studying together or in libraries. Now they had the rest of their lives together. Not much longer now, she thought.

"How about some music?" said John reaching for the radio.

"John! Watch where you're driving!"

John tried to get back into the right lane, but the wet roads made this impossible. The car hydroplaned several hundred yards sideswiping several cars before it crashed into a truck coming around the corner.

*　　*　　*

Jean Ann woke in a cold sweat. The dream had been so real. Twelve years later, the accident still came back to haunt her.

"Are you all right?" Rich asked her.

"Sorry. I didn't mean to wake you. I'll be all right."

She got up, went to the kitchen, and made herself a cup of coffee. Rich came from the bedroom to the kitchen. He stared at her for a moment before saying, "Honey, I've been concerned about you lately. These nightmares just keep waking you up every night. It's been this way all week."

"I thought that I finally had that accident off my mind."

"You have to get it off your mind. All of this grieving can't bring John back."

"He was the closest friend I ever had."

"I realize that, but you must let go of the past. You and John didn't get married. You married me."

He spoke to her gently, yet firmly, and that's what she loved about him. He was just like John that way. When John was killed, she had no other close friends.

The other kids in her childhood had never given her a hard time, but she had never developed any close friendships with them. In junior high, the two of them did make other friends, but they still preferred each other's company and their books to other kids.

*   *   *

Jean Ann sat at her typewriter finishing up the last of a novel that she had been working on, a novel about the married life of two childhood sweethearts who had the rest of their lives together. Next Wednesday would be the publishers' deadline, but she liked to have things done in advance. Even in college, the other students could never understand why she never procrastinated. At least she had always gotten everything done. That saved her the headache of cramming everything in the night before.

She typed the last page and was just putting the papers into the envelope to be mailed when she heard Rich come in the front door downstairs.

"Honey, I'm home," he called.

She hurried down to meet him.

"You're home early." She hugged him warmly.

"Our meeting broke up earlier than I thought it would. I could have stayed at the office to get some work done, but it's something that can wait. How about dinner tonight?"

"Sure. I just finished typing my work. I'll be ready in a few minutes."

They went to that Chinese restaurant, the first place they ever had dinner together. That had been five years after college graduation. Jean Ann had been rooming with Lynn who had been her college roommate. At Lynn's insistence, she had gone on a blind date with Rich.

*   *   *

"You're still trying to get over it?" Lynn asked her one night.

"How can I?"

"Why grieve this long?"

"Why are you talking about this?"

"You haven't been out with one guy since his death. All that interests you now is your work."

"Well, I'm good at my work and making money. That's what I have now."

"Well, you can have more if you want it."

Lynn thought a minute, then said, "Hey, there's someone I'd like you to meet. His name's Rich."

"I don't want to meet anyone."

"Come on! I think Rich is the person to help you get over this. I used to go with him, and I think you two will get along just great."

Jean Ann found out she and Rich had much in common. Both loved writing. Rich worked as an editor, and she had begun her first novel. Both preferred to spend evenings at home, although Rich was the more outgoing. He enjoyed going to parties.

Jean Ann had never expected anything to come out of meeting him, but Friday night of that same week, he had called her to ask her to a movie. After that, they started dating regularly. They dated for five years.

One morning during the third year they had dated, Jean Ann rushed downstairs and went to the kitchen for a quick cup of coffee before hurrying to her meeting. Lynn walked in wearing a bathrobe and slippers.

"Good morning," she yawned. "Seeing Rich tonight?"

"I don't think I'll be seeing him any more," said Jean Ann sipping coffee.

"Why not?" Lynn poured herself a cup too.

Jean Ann didn't answer that question.

"After all this time, you're still holding on to John."

"I've been seeing Rich for three years now. I think we should stop seeing each other for a while."

"So you can go back to living in the past with John. He is dead now. Accept that."

*   *   *

"Accept that," said Rich as they sat over coffee in the kitchen. "He's been dead twelve years. You know, sometimes I think you married me because you think I can give you what he did. You're expecting me to take the place of a fiance you lost years ago."

She looked at the clock. It was 3:00 in the morning. For an hour they had sat here talking like this. Another nightmare.

"You're not taking any one's place," she suddenly blurted out. "I married you because I love you."

"Maybe you do, but I remind you of John."

He had never talked to her quite like this before, telling her that she was using him to take John's place. She had almost broken up with him that one time because of that, but at Lynn's insistence had continued seeing him. After a while, she felt that she really did care for him. Was he right now?

He got up suddenly and went to the bedroom. She followed him.

"Where are you going?" she asked him when she saw him getting dressed.

"I'm going out. I don't know who you want more, John or me!"

As the front door slammed behind him, she wondered if another door had been closed in her life. She had lost John, and now wondered if she had lost Rich. Was what he told her true? Was she hoping that he would give her what John could have?

She must have dozed off because the ringing telephone jerked her back to reality. She glanced at the clock. 6:30 AM. She ran from the bedroom thinking, Oh no, please don't anything happen to Rich.

"Hello Jean," came Rich's voice.

"Rich, I've been worried. Where are you?"

"At the other side of town. I've been driving around these last few hours thinking…well… about us. I think we need some time apart."

She was stunned.

"When are you coming back?"

"I'll be in touch."

"I love you, Rich."

She hadn't told him that in a long time. There was silence at the other end of the line.

"Are you still there?" she asked.

"I'll be over to get some of my things, and I'll call you in a few days."

A few days turned into weeks, and during that time, Jean Ann often went to places Rich had taken her, favorite restaurants, movie theaters, the park they had often taken walks in. She missed him, even more than she missed John. Through him, she had become more outgoing, had made more friends. She had dreaded this at first, but later had come to enjoy a social life. Though a part of her missed John, the quiet evenings they had spent together had been replaced by parties, friends, going to movies, or taking trips with friends.

On Sunday, she heard the publishers. They wanted her novel. Jean Ann wished Rich were here to know this. Had she now lost him too? At this same time of year John had died. After twelve years, she had finally completed a novel, about the married life of two childhood sweethearts who had the rest of their lives together.

Suddenly she couldn't stand being in the town with so many memories of Rich any longer. Leaving the house, she got into her car and drove to; well, she didn't care where. For hours, she drove not realizing where until she found herself in the town where she and John had lived. She drove slowly through the streets until she came to cemetery where John lay buried. Jean Ann drove by several times before she finally parked the car across the street. She waited a few seconds before she got out.

Walking through the cemetery to his grave was not easy. She had never visited his grave since the funeral. His death and his funeral had been a dream to her, did not seem real at the time.

*   *   *

A hand touched her shoulder as she stared at the closed casket, and she turned to face Lynn.

"I'm sorry," said Lynn.

"Thank you."

"Is there any thing I can do for you?"

"I don't think so."

"I'm here for you."

"Thanks. I'll let you know if I need any thing."

She could hardly believe that she was accepting condolences from friends. It all had to be a dream.

John was buried the next day. Jean Ann stood and watched the casket lowered into the grave. Like a sleepwalker, she walked over to the flower arrangement and picked a rose. She hardly realized that she kissed it and tossed it into the grave. A few minutes later, she turned and walked back to her car.

*   *   *

After almost turning back to her car several times, she finally stood at his grave. He's gone said a voice. Accept that; move on with your life.

"It's really over," she said suddenly knowing it was her own voice that had spoken.

She had been trying to keep the past alive through Rich; yet, without realizing it, had allowed herself to live in the present with Rich. When she had realized this, she had fled back into the past again.

"It's really over," she said again and hurried away.

She had a life to live now with Rich—if he would have her back.

MOVING DAY

Julie stared at all the boxes with most of her belongings already packed in them. Might as well get this job finished, she thought. She started by packing the portable television, the clock radio, and the vanity mirror on the white chest of drawers. Not much to do there, just rolling up some wires and packing the objects into some boxes.

Some things had to be thrown out, some old school papers and notebooks, some old tennis shoes, and some mail that was no longer important.

Julie carried the bag of garbage outside to the garbage can. As she came inside to go back upstairs, she had to pass through the kitchen again. This same room in which she and Mary had spent evenings just talking. She could hear the two of them now.

*   *   *

"My grandmother's funeral is tomorrow," Julie told Mary. "I'll spend tomorrow night at my parents' house."

She had loved her grandmother and hated to face seeing her for the last time.

"You'll be back Thursday?" Mary asked her.

"Right. I don't know if I can go through this tomorrow."

"Sure you can. You'll shed a few tears, but you'll be all right. You're a Christian now and believe that she's in a better place."

"Yeah, I know she's in a better place, but still…"

"You have some fond memories of her, but don't let her death depress you. Remember that you'll see her again in the next life."

"I know, but I hope I can make it through tomorrow."

"Sure you can."

Julie started to ask her for some prayers, but the phone rang. As Mary went to answer it, she gently touched Julie's face. She's right, Julie thought going upstairs. I have to go tomorrow.

Julie did go to the funeral and saw her grandmother for the last time. During her childhood, her grandmother had been the one good thing in her life. How often Julie had wondered what she would do when she was gone.

Taking her last look at her, she felt a strength that she had never had before her conversion. Her grandmother was in a better place, and although Julie had lost her, she had other people in her life now that she could consider family, friends at college, at church, in the neighborhood, and especially Mary.

As Julie leaned over and kissed her grandmother's cheek, she knew that she would see her again.

* * *

She had roomed at Mary's for the first three years of college. Now she was lucky enough to get an apartment just as cheap until she would finish college in the spring.

The small brown, wooden jewelry box she would pack with odds and ends. Before packing it, Julie opened it and lifted out the fine chain necklace Mary had given her for Christmas. Mary had been such a friend during the time she had roomed here. She gently fondled the necklace and returned it to the box.

Receipts that Mary had written to her when she paid her rent every month she placed into an envelope. This she packed with copies of income tax forms. Julie started to pack the things on the dresser, an artificial bouquet of red roses, bottles of perfume, a brown wooden box containing her rings, and the Bible that Mary had given her after her conversion almost three years ago.

The food in the refrigerator had to be packed. In an hour, Jeff would be here to help her move. Where was Mary? Couldn't she be here to say goodbye? Maybe not. She had to shop for a stove for her new trailer. Julie went downstairs and walked through the rooms. She stood in the doorway of the living room where she and Mary had often watched television.

* * *

"You snake!" Mary exclaimed.

They were watching J.R. in one of his plots on the TV soap, Dallas.

"At least the show's not dull with him around."

"That's for sure. Want another cup of tea? You're welcome to it."

"Okay. Don't get up. I'll go get it."

Julie went to the kitchen and filled her cup from the teakettle whose water was still hot. She thought of how lucky she was. Mary was more of a friend than a landlady. For the first time in her life, she felt at home in a place. All the years of her childhood had been full of insecurities, a family that fought all the time, close relatives who were alcoholics, her own battle with drugs and alcohol. After overcoming those problems, she had enrolled in college full time and rented the remaining room in Mary's house.

"The toad's not home yet," Julie told Mary as she returned to the living room.

"No, I doubt he'll be back tonight if he's not home by now. I tell you, he prowls around like an old tomcat."

"Two at home aren't enough for him?"

"I guess not."

John, "the toad," was the other renter and was often out all night. Julie and Mary often teased him about chasing the girls. A disabled veteran and living a carefree life, he was called "the toad" behind his back because of his excess weight and sloppiness.

"He's all right," Julie told Mary. "He does favors for us."

"Yeah, but I wish he wouldn't call us the women he lives with!"

"Yeah, a woman would be pretty desperate to go to bed with that!"

*　　*　　*

"The toad" had moved out over two weeks ago. Julie went back upstairs and through her apartment checking to be sure everything was packed. Ten rooms in this house Mary had taken care of! The woman was eighty years old, and it was now too much for her. It was better that she had sold it and bought the trailer.

There was one last thing for her to do. Sitting on her bed, she wrote out a check for the rent and placed it in an envelope. Then she noticed the olive wood communion cup and the palm branch on her dresser that she had missed when packing. She picked these up, slowly walked back downstairs to the kitchen and placed the envelope, the cup, and her key on the table. Taking a pen and paper, she sat at the table. For a minute, she squeezed her eyes shut as tears came. Sighing, she wrote a few words on the paper:

> Mary, your check's in the envelope. Thanks for everything these last few years.
> Love, Julie

She could have written more, but writing goodbye was hard enough. The palm branch had to be burned. Taking it to the living room fireplace, she waited a minute before lighting a match to it.

*　　*　　*

Julie and Mary sat in the booth at Pizza Hut munching pizza.

"I'm glad you talked me into getting out for a while," said Mary. "I didn't feel like cooking my supper tonight."

"Neither did I," Julie told her.

"Do you like school better since you changed your major?"

"Sure, I like it a lot better."

"I think Spanish is a better major for you. I'm glad you decided to make the change instead of making yourself miserable."

"I'm considering a career in translation now. I think I'll like that better even though I won't be making as much money."

"Good for you! I'm glad you decided not to quit school. You won't get a good job without a college education these days."

"I know. I quit college before. I know what I want now, and I'll finish school this time."

"Well, I'm behind you all the way."

"Hey, why we go up to the mall. They're having some sales this week."

"Sounds good to me. It feels good just to get out of that house occasionally."

*　　*　　*

It was almost time to go. Julie stood looking around the living room as she waited for Jeff, her new landlord and a good friend of Mary's. He was good enough to help her move. She didn't want to go.

There was a knock at the kitchen door. He's here now, she thought and hurried to the kitchen.

"Hi," said Jeff. "Are you ready?"

She nodded. He helped her to carry her belongings downstairs and load the truck.

"It's a hard thing for you to do," he told her. "You'll make worse decisions."

"I know," she said. "I've made worse ones."

There was now one load to put in the truck.

"Do you want me to get the door?" he asked as they went outside.

She waited a few seconds.

"Yes, would you get it please?" she requested.

THE WAYSIDE

For a minute, Mr. Duvall gazed at the scenic Shenandoah landscape before entering the wayside for another day of management. He passed through the gift shop on his way to the office. Alice, the supervisor, was giving the cashiers their instructions for the day. By the end of the day, they had to have stocked an order that would be in. He noticed Bernice, who also worked in the campground, looking more tired than usual. She had been putting in a lot of overtime lately. She, Melissa, and Shelly received their instructions from Alice and went to smoke their usual cigarettes before clocking in.

He passed through the dining room, where the waitresses were arranging the tables for the day. Tammy, a new waitress, and Mary had their stations prepared and were having a smoke before work.

He went to the kitchen to get a cup of coffee. Lloyd, the head chef, was already mumbling to himself about working two jobs and having just three or four hours of sleep every night. I'll have to give him and Bernice a few days off, thought Mr. Duvall. When the Fourth of July weekend is over, things should slow down. Keith, another cashier, had called in sick earlier. Mr. Duvall offered to man a register when he had the time. The cashiers were busy all day. There would be a fifteen-minute rush of customers and one or two minutes of peace before another rush. In addition to this, the cashiers had to stock over a thousand dollars worth of souvenirs. Bernice manned the souvenir register while Mr. Duvall manned the food register. Alice priced the souvenirs while Shelly and Melissa stocked them. If there were too many customers in line, one had to go help by bagging the souvenirs.

At 12:00 Melissa offered to man the register while Bernice took her lunch break. Bernice joined Lloyd in the employee break room.

"I'm sick of these customers," she complained. "You get those that think they're the only customers to be waited on."

"Just be glad you're not in the kitchen. Things get really hectic back here."

"Well, at least you're not out with the customers."

"If you were in my place, you wouldn't last long."

Lloyd put out his cigarette and returned to the kitchen.

"Hey, Bob!" he yelled. "Get those dishes done!"

"I will when I get this floor mopped."

"Forget the floor! Those dishes need washed!"

Bob went to the sink to do the pile of dishes.

"A hamburger and fries to go," said Tammy at the carry-out window.

"Wait till I get caught up," said Marilyn at the grill. "I'm two orders behind."

"The customer's in a hurry."

"That's his problem."

"Marilyn," said Lloyd who was stirring a kettle of soup at the stove. "Get that carry-out order ready, and get the other two later!"

Marilyn cursed under her breath and put a hamburger on the grill.

"You're going to catch me in the wrong mood sometime!" Lloyd snapped.

"No matter," said Marilyn under her breath. "I'm not coming back tomorrow anyway."

She got the order ready and handed it to Tammy who walked toward the door of the dining room where the man was waiting. On her way over, a woman asked her why her order was taking so long.

"It's been a busy day," said Tammy. "It should only be a few more minutes."

"Well, I don't have all day!"

"Your order will be ready in a little while."

She hurried over to the man waiting for his carryout order.

"It's about time! I've had service a lot quicker than this!"

He went to the food register that Mr. Duvall was manning. Mr. Duvall rang him up and called Tammy over.

"Don't worry about it," he told her. "We get customers like that occasionally."

"It's just not my day."

"The first few days are always the worst. You're doing a good job."

"Thanks."

"Just hang in there. After the holiday, it'll get better."

"Tammy," called Mary. "You have some customers."

Tammy went to wait on them. Mr. Duvall manned the food register for the rest of the afternoon. The waitresses cleaned their stations and clocked out. Shelly, Melissa, and Alice clocked out. Bernice stayed to work the late shift. Mr. Duvall went to the office to work on some bookkeeping. He had some good employees. Why couldn't the customers realize that they did their jobs? He looked at his watch; another hour to go. He had been working for thirty minutes when Bernice asked him to come help with a line of customers. He reopened the food register to wait on some. They closed at 8:00. Bernice was overworked, but he needed her to work tomorrow. She would have some time off when the pace slowed down a little. He lit up a cigarette and drove home to rest for another day of work.

POSSESSION

She was giving her apartment its once-a-week cleaning. She stood on the chair to dust above the doorframes and windows. She moved objects to dust under them, her portable black and white television set that she watched no more than a few hours a week, her white vanity mirror, her bottles of perfume, her small brown wooden jewelry boxes, and her bouquet of artificial red roses. These objects she took the time to dust. He had often complimented her on her neatness.

He was ten years her senior and so attractive. Sometimes he would come to see her every day, and other times she wouldn't see him for at least a week. She remembered how his strong arms often held her close to him as she stood resting her head on his chest and his large hands gently caressing her. This always led to gentle loving.

He was gone now; had been gone for a month. He had finally found a better paying job and moved only thirty minutes away from her. Nothing like this will happen to me again, she thought and began sorting through some mail that had been laying around. Some of it had to be thrown out, some old newsletters from her church, some old circulars, and some old post cards from old friends. She came across his new address that he had left for her and crumpled it. She started to throw it into the wastebasket, then hesitated. She tossed it onto the table next to the pile of letters concerning her work in the national parks. She reread the one informing her about her next position.

Another month yet before she would leave for this one. Maybe he wouldn't be back. Then again, if he said he would return, he would unless his work kept him away. She glanced around the room and noticed a few objects that she had missed when dusting, the small olive wood communion cup, the small plastic set of praying hands, and the small wooden cross. She picked these up and gently dusted them. Gently she fondled and kissed the cross before setting it on the dresser.

She had to vacuum the rug. Moving chairs and end tables, she swept every inch of the room. She still needed to clean the bathroom. She scrubbed the shower, the sink, and the toilet before scrubbing the floor. Returning to her living room, she set up her ironing board. A lot of ironing to do this week, her light blue blouse with the ruffles, her light pink blouse that she always wore with her pearls, her green plaid pantsuit, her white blouse that she always wore under her brown, blue, and gray sweaters. A pile of wrinkled blouses that she wore for everyday still lay on the floor. No sense fussing with these, she thought and hung them in the closet.

He had always thought she was such a lady. He once told her that she was all his and would never let another man near her. She shuddered as she remembered the last time she had tried telling him that it was over and how he wouldn't let her go. She should have known better; after all the bar fights he had been in, all the men he had beaten up, men drunk enough to dare fighting him.

She put away her ironing board and glanced at the clock. 5:30. Another day almost over. Might as well eat something. She had her supper and went to bathe. She looked over herself. The bruises had all healed by now. Sighing she lay back in the tub enjoying the warmth of the water.

Twenty minutes later she returned to her bedroom to do her hair. As she ran the comb through her hair, there was a knock at the door. It was probably the neighbor across the hall needing something. She hurried to the living room, opened the door, and went pale as she realized that it had not ended.

No Sympathy Please

I've ruined my life at the age of twenty-one by using pot, all hard drugs, and alcohol. Nurses come to my room with my medication and talk to me, but they are far away. I barely hear them, but I make myself answer when they ask how I am. Once a day, an aide comes to take me to my sessions with Dr. Stone who encourages me to be open with him, which I try, but it's not easy. I asked him yesterday if I'll ever be well, but he didn't know. In an hour, that aide will be here to take me to see him.

I'm sure you're wondering how I got into this mess. I'll tell you, not for sympathy, but because Dr. Stone encourages me to be free of it.

I was an average kid, living in a blue-collar neighborhood. I remember my mother, but I never knew my father. I've been told he died in an auto accident when I was two. After his death, my mother tried to support her and me by working as a hotel maid. I was too young to understand her problem with a heart murmur. My earliest memories are of her coming home from work very tired and often complaining of chest pains. However, she always managed to spend time with me, playing games, telling me stories, and an occasional trip to the park.

I got up one morning to find paramedics carrying my mother out on a stretcher. I never had a chance to say goodbye. A neighbor and his wife took me to stay with them. Those were long nights for me when I would lie awake staring at a nightlight. I would wake up in the morning confused and go through every room searching. The neighbor woman would take me to the park every afternoon where I spent more time looking for my mother than playing.

One day she held me on her lap and gently told me my mother was in Heaven.

"What's Heaven?" I asked.

"It's where God is, and your mother is with Him."

I didn't know what that meant, but I somehow knew I would never see my mother again.

I went to stay with people I had never seen before. A woman that never smiled and was always too busy to look at me took my mother's place. Her husband left every morning with a briefcase, and I never saw him again until the next morning. I soon learned to stay out of that woman's way when she often told me what a bother I was. My days were spent either in my room with picture books or exploring the back yard.

I started elementary school, and having a natural curiosity about everything, I soon became a top pupil. The other kids envied me for this and avoided me. My books became my only friends.

It went that way until I entered junior high. I noticed the other kids using dope, and they looked so free. One day I was walking home from school and passed Julie, a new girl, smoking a joint.

"Hi," she called. "Want a hit?"

What would it be like? Pretending it was natural for me, I took a few hits. After one joint I felt exuberant, free.

"You're Lynn, right?"

"Yeah."

"Live around here?"

"Just up the street."

"I've seen you in school. Want to come over to my place for a while?"

"Sure."

Julie had plenty of stash hidden in her room.

"Hey Lynn, can I buy some angel dust from you?"

"I don't have any stash," I said before I thought.

Julie stared at me, then grinned.

"Well, I didn't start on anything until last year. We'll take care of this."

For the first time in years, I felt free. Julie showed me where I could buy stash, and I soon learned that pot and hash together give a good head buzz. Drinking, smoking, and hard drugs soon followed. It wasn't hard to get away with it because my teachers thought I was a good example for other students, and my foster parents never cared what I did. While I still loved my books and kept my grades up, I still wanted a good high several times a day.

Graduation Day came. Undecided about a career, I registered in a general studies program at a community college. I decided not to take classes that summer and just enjoy my last summer as a kid. To support my habit, I had been working part-time as a cashier. Now I worked full-time and bought even more stash.

I couldn't understand why I still felt depressed every time I came down from a high. Neither could I understand why I so often felt so far away from everyone else even in a crowded room. I could see and hear everyone else, but I wasn't really there. To keep myself close to everyone and not so depressed, I got high more often.

My classes started in the fall. I had gotten a scholarship that covered part of my tuition. With the help of a loan, I paid the rest and got my books. My foster parents decided it was time for me to move out, so I rented a cheap apartment in a dilapidated building and continued working part-time. After two weeks, I dropped down to a part-time student because I needed more money.

I enjoyed my classes. High school had been too easy for me; so college was more of a challenge. Chemistry was my favorite class because I enjoyed mixing up compounds and learning more about the chemical reactions in our environment. My professor eventually noticed my interest and asked me to work part-time as his assistant.

Christmas break came, and I had finished my first term with 3.4 average. My foster parents had never once visited me after I moved out and never bothered to ask me over for Christmas. During the break, I cashiered full-time. On weekends, I went to parties. I would leave my apartment for work Friday morning and go to a party that same night. Sunday afternoon I would come home to crash until going to work in the morning.

Christmas Day I spent alone. Nobody was having any parties because everyone I knew had other places to go. I spent the day at home shooting myself up with smack. I remembered my mother. I remembered the afternoons we spent together in the park and the evenings that we spent playing games at home. I remembered some pre-school friends that I often met in the park. Finally I thought of the last time I saw my mother and felt anger toward her and toward my foster parents. Some laughter in the next apartment brought me to reality. Some Christmas music was playing, and I heard children playing and comparing their gifts. I looked toward the bathroom where I kept some pills and a few razors.

My classes started again in January. This term I couldn't concentrate on my classes too well. When my professors lectured, they seemed far away from me. I'd go home in the evening and try to study, but my mind wandered. I was controlled by my need for drugs. I would try unsuccessfully not to get high for hours at a time. I eventually started hearing voices when I was home and would turn to look. Nobody would be there.

Somehow I managed to passes that term. I went to work full-time that summer. No peace there. Customers always wanting something. Crying children. One day in July, my boss called me to his office and demanded to know what was wrong with me.

"This is the third customer this week that said you overcharged him!"

I stared at him.

"I've also had complaints from customers that you were rude to them!"

Again I said nothing as I felt my mind drifting off. Then I heard voices. Angry voices. I couldn't understand what they were saying. I glanced around the room.

"What's wrong with you?"

"I don't know," I managed to say.

He stared at me a long minute, then softened.

"You have been putting in a lot of over-time lately. Go home and rest. I'll have someone relieve you."

I didn't come back to work the next day. The following week, I got a job working as a hotel maid.

I went back to college that fall as a chemistry major, but after the first semester, I dropped out and worked full-time. I was only twenty and using every drug I could get my hands on.

Over the next year, I would go to work high or drunk and come home the same way. I started keeping stash and a bottle hidden at work. I was just drifting through life and constantly fighting the urge to kill myself. I don't know how many times I got out the razor and ran it over my wrist imagining the pain. I heard voices at home and at work telling me to end it all.

On Christmas Eve of my twenty-first year, I was cleaning my hotel rooms when my supervisor confronted me.

"Lynn, I found this in your cart outside."

I saw the bottle in her hand but didn't say anything.

"I've suspected this for weeks. Your work's been sloppy, and I've had some complaints from guests about the way you talk to them!"

I stared at her mutely.

She sighed and told me, "Go on home, but don't come back."

I went home and crashed on my bed. Hearing Christmas carolers down the street, I got up and went to the window. Mothers were taking their children to every house on the street. Suddenly I saw myself with my own mother years earlier. I saw the old neighborhood, and a bunch of us kids walking with our mothers down the street. We went to every house on the block singing carols. Sometimes someone would give us candy. Once someone invited us in for hot chocolate.

Christmas Day my mother and I always spent together. I remembered our last Christmas together as I sat on her lap while she read 'Twas the Night Before Christmas. I remember her loving look as I opened the gifts she had managed to buy for me.

I saw myself walking toward the bathroom and opening the medicine cabinet to get out the razor. I barely felt the pain as the blade tore my flesh. I ran the blade up my arm and stood watching myself bleed. Then everything went black.

I woke up hours later here in the hospital. Another tenant I had shared the bathroom with had found me. I've been here three months, but it seems longer than that. I see nobody except Dr. Stone, the nurses, and the aides. I'll go talk to Dr. Stone. I'll try to be open with him, but it won't be easy.

CITY LIFE

Boxes full of Kathy's belongings littered the apartment, but outside the day was sunny. It was hard to resist a walk, and anyway, she had to call her foster father, who was all the family she had, to let him know that she was back from Shenandoah.

She went down the dark stairway not meeting any other tenant. She left the dilapidated apartment building and walked onto Horner Street. As she walked, she passed groups of teen-agers in worn-out jeans and holey T-shirts. People running errands or going to work passed by in cars. No eye contact was made with anyone. If it was made, it was only a second before they looked away. Kathy thought of the place she had worked at over the summer. Those mountain people knew everyone else's business. They could make a person miserable if they disliked him, but they could also make him feel like one of their big family.

Kathy walked on down the street to the business section. People wearing business suits were hurrying to their destinations. On into Franklin Street where there were more people going about their business.

She made her way to a pay phone. Although her foster father never said much, she needed just a few minutes to talk to him. After the third ring, he answered, sounding depressed.

"Hello."

"Hi, it's Kathy. I just got back to town."

"Yeah!" he said sounding more cheerful. "I was going to come over today, but I thought you might be in school."

"I was home today. Wednesday and Friday afternoons and weekends I'm home."

"Son of a gun. Tell you what, I have a doctor's appointment on Friday, and I'll try to come over then. If not, I'll be over on Wednesday."

"All right, I'll be there."

"I missed you a lot."

"I missed you too."

"Take care, sweetie."

"Bye."

Kathy turned to go back into the sunshine.

A Matter of Time

It has been two months. She walks downtown to work, always looking at blue Chevrolets and pedestrians hoping to see him. Evenings she spends watching TV or reading, but always listening for his knock. ("I'll be back to get you.")

For over a year, they had been lovers. Who would have thought of them so close? So wild, she was afraid of him. Well know for his violent temper. ("He wouldn't pay me back when I went to talk to him. That's when I threw him down the steps.")

Yet, he was a gentle lover and the best friend to her by giving her all the love she needed. ("The day we met, I knew you needed someone to take care of you.") She had finally put together a life after leaving that family that only gave her insecurity and self-hate. Then she met him. ("Do you want to tell me about it?") She had told him about her childhood and later the battle with alcohol. ("I'll give you all the love you need.")

His job took him to another town. ("I'll have to leave you for a while.") She had to stay to finish college. Now, she could only wait.

THE OFFICE

The furniture in her apartment is second hand and is as old as the house. Yet, it is not shabby and makes the apartment look homey. The carpeting in the bedroom is a light tan, and no trash lies strewn across the floor. No dust has accumulated anywhere, and there are places for all of her belongings.

Next to her bed stands the nightstand made with light brown wood. Occupying the lower shelf in one pile are a beat-up college dictionary, a worn-out folder of old psychology notes, a college catalogue, the recent issue of a college literary magazine, a much used medical encyclopedia/dictionary, and, on top of that, a battered deck of cards. Next to that pile lie a medical microbiology book, a Merck Manual, and two paperback psychology books with the covers coming off.

Near the front of the dresser top lies the Good News Bible, a gift given to her by her landlady when she gave her life to the Lord two years ago. The recent issues of The Upper Room and Daily Bread are lying on top of the Bible. These she reads daily. Next to the Bible lies a large brown envelope containing information and application material for full-time mission work when she graduates next year.

The mirror hanging above her dresser has on the bottom a certificate of membership that she received when she joined the church sixteen months ago. Next to this is a small white sign with black lettering saying, "Look up and live with Christ." An arrow at the top of the sign points to a cross made from palm branches at the top of the mirror.

On the white chest of draws stands a portable black and white television set that she watches no more than a few hours a week. Next to the television set stands a clock radio set for 6:30 AM on school days and turned to the station 96.5 FM. A white vanity mirror, that her mother gave her for a birthday gift, stands behind the clock radio. On her bed lies a green pillow with a white flower design that she once made when she had nothing else to do.

On the wall above her bed hangs a calendar with most of the days filled in with appointments and meetings. Along the wall next to her bed hang white plaques, each one with a different picture of a flower arrangement. A palm branch lies across the tops of these.

This is the room that is at times more like an office to her than a bedroom. She spends most of her time in this room when she is not in class, at a meeting, or an appointment. In this room, she studies, works on activities she is involved in, or spends time with God.

VACATION

The sound of traffic outside. The quietness of the apartment. She sighed as she put her book aside and went to the kitchen for a soda. A whole month before she started her next position in the national parks. A week earlier, she had just finished her winter term classes. She had done her spring cleaning during the first week. Now there was not much to do except to pack her belongings into storage except what she would need for the summer. Might as well renew my CPR certificate at the Red Cross and try completing a first aide class as well, she thought.

She returned to her living room and turned on the TV. Turning the dial to several stations, she found one of the few programs she sometimes saw.

Glancing at her calendar filled with meetings and appointments, she realized that she hadn't changed it from March to April. Tearing off the month of March, she crumpled it and tossed it into the wastebasket. Sitting back in her chair, she watched an hour of TV before turning it off.

She turned on her radio and settled down to write a letter to a friend she hadn't written to in months. She told her about how school had gone this past term, about her next position, and her plans for continuing this work after graduating in December. She addressed and stamped the envelope and played solitaire until midnight. Not feeling tired, she got out her book and read until 2:00 AM. Putting away the book, and turning off the radio, she went to bed. The traffic outside was not so heavy now. Getting out of bed, she pressed the sleep button on the clock radio. For a few minutes, she lay staring at the ceiling before turning over on her side. As she drifted off, she thought about doing some volunteer work until May.

Transition

The moonlight streamed through the window and onto the figure under the covers. She suddenly sat up and stared around the dark room knowing she had called out his name in her sleep. She felt the desire rise in her again. She got up, turned on the light, and lit a cigarette.

This work always kept Francine on the move from one national park to another. She had always dated someone everywhere she went, but no relationship lasted. Then she had met Mark during her past college year back home. Before meeting him, she had always thought she would be a career woman and was sure he was only another man in her travels. Now she wondered if this move had been right.

She put out her cigarette, turned out the light, and crawled back under the covers.

The next day at work lasted longer than usual because Francine wasn't feeling well.

"Francine," said Doris, the supervisor. "Would you please go down to the stock room and see if we have any more of those Teddy bear puppets?"

"Sure."

Glad for a break, she went to the stock room, and, for a minute, leaned against the shelves as a feeling of lightheadedness came to her. She looked through the boxes, but couldn't find any more puppets. The rest of the day went slowly. A man, his wife, and three small children came into the gift shop. The youngest daughter picked out an Indian bracelet and brought it to the register. As she looked for her money, her father offered to buy it for her. Doris said, "Children are a blessing."

"Yes, they sure are," he said and put his face down to his daughter's.

She kissed his cheek. Francine felt envious as she watched them leave. She went home from work feeling more tired than usual. She slept restlessly all night. More than once, she came to the edge of consciousness to feel a soreness in her throat.

The alarm went off at 6:00. Aware of her sore throat and feeling nauseated, she stumbled across the room to turn off the alarm. Francine dressed in everyday clothes and went to the office. Neil was the manager on duty that day.

"Can I take today off? I got up sick this morning."

"Sure, I understand. Go home and rest, and I'll have someone come down later to check on you."

Francine went to her dorm room and lay in bed, but found it hard to rest. For an hour, she lay awake wishing she could be back home.

She was just starting to doze off when there was a knock on her door. She stumbled out of bed to answer it.

"Hi, Francine. I came to check on you," said John who worked the front desk and was a good friend.

"I'm hanging in there."

"Can I get you anything?" John asked sitting down.

"Would you mind getting me a sandwich later?"

"No problem. I'll just get it when I go on lunch break."

Francine lay back on the pillows and asked, "Has it been very busy today?"

"No, it's been slow all morning. It should be slow all week."

"Maybe I can just ask for a few days off."

"You should. I'll even take you to the doctor if you need to go."

John glanced over at a picture of Mark on the dresser.

"You really should call your boyfriend a little later. It'll lift your spirits."

"We had an agreement."

"I know that, but I can see you miss him. Anyway, he probably misses you."

"Maybe I'll try a little later."

"Good. I better get back to work. See you later."

After John left, she lay back on her pillows and tried to sleep again. Call Mark. She hadn't talked to him since before coming down here. They had agreed that some time apart to date others would be good for them. Did he miss her as much as she missed him? Did he still feel the same about her?

Francine later went to see Neil about a few days off.

"Take six days off. We'll have Claire work your shifts for you. If you need to see a doctor, let us know."

"Thanks, I really appreciate this."

"No problem. You just take care of yourself."

For the next six days, Francine rested, sat on the porch, and went on walks. She tried to reach Mark several times, but never got an answer. She began to feel uneasy.

One evening when she was sitting on the porch, John stopped by.

"How are you doing?"

"A lot better. How about you?"

"Couldn't be better! My girlfriend, Mary, was up yesterday. You know we were talking about getting married. Well, we finally decided to tie the knot."

"Congratulations!"

John looked at her a minute.

"Have you called Mark yet?"

"I've tried several times, but he hasn't been home."

"Well, keep trying. You'll get him at home eventually."

Francine glanced at her watch and said, "About time for supper."

"I hope they're have some real food tonight."

"Yeah, how can I get better if they don't give me good food?"

After supper, Francine went to the phone in the back office and dialed the operator.

"Operator."

"Hello, I'd like to make a time and charges call to 814-255-2831."

The phone only rang three times before Mark answered.

"Hello."

"Hi Mark. It's me."

"Francine. How have you been?"

"Well, I've been off sick these last few days, but I'll be back to work the day after tomorrow."

"That's always rough. How have you been otherwise?"

"Good. Work is good, and the people are great to work with. There are plenty of places to go on my days off. How have you been?"

"Good. I had some vacation time from work, and I visited my parents all week. We had some relatives over for a family reunion."

"You'll have to come down some weekend."

"Yeah, I'll have to do that. I've missed you a lot."

"I've missed you too."

"How much longer do you have to work there?"

"Only about two months yet."

"Well, I'll be down to see you before then."

"I think this will be my last season I'll be doing this work."

"Are you sure that's what you want?"

"Yes."

"I'll try to be down next weekend."

"All right, I'll see you then."

"Take care, sweetie."

"You too. Bye."

After the operator told her the amount, Francine held the receiver a minute and, her hand shaking, slowly hung up. She went to pay Jane the amount.

BURNOUT

She snuggled under the covers letting the blackness of the room envelope her. She tried to fall asleep, but the throbbing in her head kept her awake. Worse than the headache was that her mind was still at work.

Try to relax, she told herself. Six days off to get caught up on rest. She thought of Jesse and knew that he missed her as she missed him. Why did she continue working in the national parks when she had met him? She now realized that that she was tired of this moving around with no roots anywhere.

A knock at the door jerked her to reality. She stumbled out of bed to answer it.

"Hi, I came to check on you," said Mike entering the dark room and glancing around uneasily.

"Why don't you let some sunshine in here? It's like a tomb."

She didn't protest as he opened the drapes and raised the window. Some sunlight broke through the blackness.

"How are you doing?"

"I'm hanging in there."

"Can I get you anything?"

"If you don't mind, I'd like some lunch later."

"No problem, I'll just get it from the kitchen."

She stared at her co-worker in the ministry a minute.

"I hate to stick you with all the work."

"Don't worry about it. You just get better."

Mark pulled up a chair. She lay back on her pillows wishing he'd leave.

"I really think you should call your parents or your boyfriend."

"I'll try to reach them later on."

"Good. I think it'll lift your spirits."

Mark glanced around the room at her clothes and some dirty dishes everywhere and shook his head. He looked through the blackness in the room at the brightness outside.

"Hey, want to come outside and sit on the porch?"

"I'd rather sleep."

"You sure?"

"Yeah."

"All right," said Mark getting up. "I'll bring you some lunch a little later."

"Okay, thanks for stopping by."

"You bet!"

After Mark left, she went to the window and closed the drapes. Yes, close out all those responsibilities and the people she had to deal with. She lay back down and let the blackness surround her again.

Home Again

The house was still the same. Everything was in its usual place as it had been when I left for North Carolina. There were those plants still growing in the kitchen window. The orange tablecloth was still on the kitchen table, and the radio was still kept on a shelf behind the table. Odds and ends were still kept on the shelves below the shelf holding the radio. A bowl of fruit was still kept on the counter, and in front of that, there were still the cards that had thoughts for the day. Family pictures still hung on the walls, giving the place a cheerful appearance. Mary, my landlady, was still the same. She was seventy-nine, but she did not look that age. An active life had kept her young both in appearance and in spirit. She was now dressed in old clothes to do the work around the house. She was still able to take care of a ten-room house without any help. Things had not changed in this house, and yet, when Mary and I embraced in her kitchen, I knew that nothing was the same. In this house, I had grown emotionally and become a stronger person. This was still the same kitchen Mary and I often sat in and talked, sometimes for hours. Sometimes we would laugh and joke, and at other times, she would tell me about her family and how close they had been. Although we were strangers when we first met, we came to know each other intimately. That had been a time for me to learn what it was like to feel like part of a family.

I went upstairs to my apartment. The person who had used my apartment in my absence had made no changes in the way my belongings were arranged. The artificial flowers were still on my dresser, and above the dresser was the mirror that still had on the cross made from a palm branch. That pillow that I had made with a flower design was still on my bed. Some old school books and clothing were still in the back of my closet in the kitchen. A fern plant was still growing in my kitchen window. Yet, things were not the same as they had been when I left. This was the same apartment I had lived in for two years, the first place I ever really considered home. These rooms are like the rest of the house, plastered walls that are now cracking and second-hand furniture. Yet, the rooms are kept clean and have a homey appearance to them. Nothing has changed in this house, but I have changed since I have been away. I have continued to grow emotionally and become a stronger person just as the plants in our kitchens have continued to grow.

WHY ME?

She has never seen him before, but she knows he's out there, watching her every move. She can imagine what he is like, tall, dark, masculine, and maybe handsome.

The phone rings. She knows it is him, even before she answers the phone.

"Did you get the pictures I sent you?"

She knows his deep voice.

"What do you want from me?"

That evil laugh. She slams down the receiver. She grabs the manila envelope lying on the coffee table and throws it into the fireplace. She watches the pictures burn but knows that won't be the end of it.

Work seemed endless that day. Customers complaining, crying children, long lines at the registers. She wonders if she should leave town. Start a new life.

She feels a tap on her shoulder.

"You have a phone call," says the manager. "This is the last time I watch the register for you. Tell your male friend not to call here again."

She feels the hair rise on her neck as she goes to the office.

"Hi, Foxy Lady! You'll find more pictures when you get home. You and Jack were really hot that night!"

"What do you want from me?"

"You'll know soon enough. We'll meet, when you least expect it."

"I'll call the cops."

"That wouldn't be smart if you value your life."

Again that familiar laugh. The click at the other end. She holds the dead receiver for a minute. She will leave town. Telling the manager that there is an emergency, she hurries from the store. The phone is ringing as she enters her house.

"It won't be good to leave town, Foxy Lady, because I'll be right behind you."

She slams the receiver. She leaves in the middle of the night. I have to take the chance, she thought. How far she drove she didn't know. At daybreak she checks into a hotel.

Waking up in mid-afternoon, she feels refreshed, more than she had in weeks. She showers and changes clothes. She'll eat before going on.

As she goes outside, she hears footsteps behind her. She knows the evil laugh. Before she can turn around, she feels his hand over her mouth. Then the familiar voice in her ear.

"I told you I'm right behind you."

INNER STRENGTH

Who am I, this stranger lying on a gurney in the emergency room? Who are my family and friends? Doctors and nurses come to ask me questions that I don't have the answers for. Just hours ago, I knew who I was, but yet I was scared about something terrible that had happened. Yet, what happened to me? What was I running from?

I remember meeting a lady on the street who checked my purse for I.D. She found my social security card and a card for me from someone named Rick. She noticed my diamond and wedding band and felt that Rick must be my husband. She drove me here where I have been for hours.

A policeman came to talk to me. He found a card in my purse with names and phone numbers to contact in case of emergencies. Rick's name was there. He left leaving me alone with my thoughts.

Through my fear, I sensed a loving presence in the room with me, the presence of someone who filled my heart with love, the presence of someone that loved and protected me. Please help me, I found myself crying out inside.

I heard voices. I heard one familiar voice saying, "She's been losing touch with reality for two weeks now."

A nurse came into the room with a handsome, familiar-looking man.

"Do you know him?" she asked.

"He looks familiar," I said.

He stepped up to me and said, "I'm Rick, your husband. You're the love of my life."

He showed me his golden wedding band with diamonds in it identical to mine.

"Do we have any kids?" I asked him.

"I have five, and you have a six-year-old daughter."

"Why aren't they here now?"

"They don't live with us."

He started looking through my purse.

"I'm looking for your parents' phone number."

He found the card and said he'd be back. Again that familiar presence, telling me everything would be all right.

The nurse came in to check my blood pressure.

"Anything coming back to you yet?"

I shook my head.

Rick came back to say that my parents, sister, and brother-in-law would be right over. I saw him brush a tear from his eye. I had a good feeling about this man, a feeling that we must share a special relationship. Yet, there was that fear about something terrible that had happened.

"Something terrible happened," I told him.

"What happened? You can tell me."

"I don't remember," I told him.

An attractive older woman in a blue coat came in followed by a young pregnant woman and handsome young man.

"Who are you?" I asked her.

"I'm your mother."

She started to come closer.

"Now don't scare her," Rick said. "She doesn't know me."

I noticed the photo album the pregnant woman carried.

"Do you know me?" she asked.

I had no answer.

"If you don't, that's okay. I'm your sister, Diane. I'm six months pregnant. This is my husband, Don. I thought some pictures might bring back some memories for you."

"Something terrible happened," I said.

"She said that before," Rick said. "That concerns me."

"You don't remember anything?" my mother asked me.

"No," I said.

That familiar presence seemed to cry out inside, "You know me!"

Diane handed me a photo album. I opened it and noticed some black and white pictures of a Saint Bernard.

"That's Major," Diane said.

"Do you still have him?" I asked her.

"No, he just got too big to handle, and we had to give him away."

They showed me other pictures, some of children on their way to school. They told me that was my brother, sister, and some of our friends as kids. Other pictures were those of relatives that gave me a good feeling when I looked at them.

Two women entered the room. One said they would be taking me for MRI's of my head.

"She doesn't remember anything yet," Rick said.

They wheeled me to the elevator and took me to the MRI room.

"Do you think you are claustrophobic?" one asked me.

"No," I said.

They put earplugs into my ears and had me lie down on a narrow table that slid into a tube.

I lay in the tube listening to the noise of the machinery trying to remember things. Then I remembered having a bad argument with someone. Who was it? What was the argument about?

I felt the table being slid out of the tube.

"We'll be taking you back to ER," one lady who had brought me here told me.

Once back in ER, I mentioned the argument to Rick.

"What was it about?" he asked.

"I don't know."

He took my mother aside and told her, "We had an argument earlier."

"About what?"

"About our finances and the home we're building. I got too hot under the collar, and she ran out on me."

I didn't hear anything more as they walked out of the room. Was this the same man who claimed to have such a good life with me? Why would he scare me like that? That fear came back to me. Was this what I had been running from? Again that familiar presence. It wasn't the presence of another person, but rather a Superior Being. Someone who is above humanity. This Being kept telling me that everything was going to be all right; that I was in a safe place; that nobody could hurt me here.

I heard their voices again.

"I have been getting on her case a lot about little things not being done right," I heard Rick say. "But I have been so stressed out about getting this loan for our home."

"Excuse me," I heard another voice say. "Her MRI's came back normal. She will be admitted. Since your are her husband, you will need to sign some papers."

Diane and Don came in to say they had been in the coffee shop and asked me if I wanted to look at more pictures.

The doctor came in to say that I had been admitted and that they would be taking me to the psychiatric ward. At least I wouldn't be going back to some terrible situation. Rick and my mother came back in.

"You'll be all right," she said putting her hand on my shoulder.

"Yeah, we all love you and will be over to see you tomorrow," Rick said.

Diane and Don said they would bring some more pictures tomorrow. Suddenly, I saw myself sitting in a church with Rick, again feeling that presence.

"Are you remembering something?" Rick asked.

"I remember God."

THE SUMMER OF '85

"These cabins don't look like much, but they're safe," said Tammy.

"Yes," I said. "Bruce said that they're safe."

I had just arrived and was looking at what was to be my home until September. It was May 9, 1985, and September seemed a long way off. There were three cabins, the laundromat, and the Old Pisgah Inn all of which housed the employees. The wooden gray buildings were a dull gray color appropriate for the weather that day, dull gray skies and drizzle. Never having been that far south before, I was on the Blueridge Parkway in North Carolina, and I wondered what kind of summer that I would have. Sure I would make friends, but they would all end up in the past like others I had known. It has always been that way with me.

There was no time to think about the summer ahead. Tammy led me into a cabin almost across the paved path from the laundromat. We walked down a hallway that was a slight maze and to a single bedroom on the left.

"You'll probably get a roommate later on in the season when we get busier," she told me.

She helped me carry my luggage in and told me that she would be back in thirty to forty-five minutes to check on me. So this was where I would live. The room was dull-looking, but when I had settled in, it took on a homey appearance. Two walls were paneled, and the other two were white plaster. The carpeting was a faded green. One section of the room, to be used for closet space, was closed off with a faded beige curtain. A bed stood in one corner, a dresser stood against one wall, and two lamps stood at each end of the room.

I later went to the main office to ask when I would report to work the next day. That was when I met Mrs. O'Connell, one of the owners of the inn.

"I talked to Romaine," she said stiffly. "Report to work at nine o'clock tomorrow morning."

"What is the job?" I asked.

"Housekeeping."

Then she went on with her work. No words of welcome. Sure she was my employer, but that was not the warmest welcome I had received from anyone.

By nighttime, I was settled in and ready to report to work in the morning. Housekeeping! I had never been much of a housekeeper before. How would this work out? No matter! I had some income for the summer, and I could try to save some money to continue college in the fall.

Mt. Pisgah Inn was divided into three sections, A, B, and C buildings. The A building is the smallest with five rooms plus the main office downstairs. The day after my arrival was my first day at work. This was the first day that I walked the five-minute walk from my room down to the C building. I then had to go up to the second floor linen room to report for work. There was some laughing behind the door. This must be the right place I thought and knocked.

"Come in," said several voices.

I entered the small linen room. A small sink was on my left as I entered, and along the left wall were shelves well stocked with linens and bathroom articles. A cart carrying supplies for the rooms, a cart for dirty linen, and a wastebasket with wheels took up a good portion of the room. Not much room was left at the other end of the room for the small card table around which sat five women and a man.

"I'm looking for Romaine," I said.

"I'm her," said a petite woman with light brown hair.

"My name's Sara Kemp. I'm reporting for work."

"Oh yeah, Mrs. O'Connell said I would be getting a new girl."

Introductions were made. There were Shirley, an older woman in her fifties, Cheryl, who was Shirley's daughter-in-law, Beverly, a girl about twenty, and Irene, a pleasant middle-aged woman. There was also Gerald, Romaine's husband, who worked as the handyman. Romaine was the head housekeeper and seemed easy to work for. Well, I had gotten a warmer welcome than I had the previous day from Mrs. O'Connell.

"Do you have any experience working as a maid?" Romaine asked me.

"No, I don't," I said.

"Cheryl, take her with you today, and show her the ropes."

I had done hard work before but never like the work in housekeeping. A lot of heavy lifting and pulling was involved. The carts were heavy to pull when they were full of supplies. Not only did we clean the hotel rooms and supply clean linens and bathroom supplies, there were also odd jobs to be done, such as cleaning the employees' bathrooms and laundromat, picking up trash on the grounds, and cleaning the office. When doing jobs at the employees' quarters, we had to carry everything needed to work with, which included trash bags, towels, cleaning rags, bottles of cleaning fluids, a broom, and vacuum cleaner. I was the maid who ended up doing these jobs once a week.

The work was hard enough, but our employers ruled over us like Prussian dictators. They expected everything to be done to perfection and were quick to fire anyone who failed to do this or who broke the rules. Except for a ten o'clock curfew for noise and visitors, we were free to do as we pleased when off the clock. The O'Connell's, the managers and our employers, were strict perfectionists who expected the best from employees even though they were just new on the job. The turnover rate was very high. Many employees didn't last long because they either quit or were fired. When fired, they were given ten minutes to get all their belongings together and get off the mountain. It didn't take much to get fired. For instance, one employee who had worked in the coffee shop was fired because he did not charge a customer for cheese on his hotdog. Another lady was fired because she asked to do more besides waitress work. She had been employed there for five years.

There were three in the O'Connell family, Thomas, Phyllis, and their son Bruce. Since I was in housekeeping, I worked directly under Mrs. O'Connell, and she was the one I got to know over the summer. She sometimes inspected the rooms. I went to work one morning, and Romaine had gotten a note from her. Romaine informed all of us that dust had been found under the TV sets. For several days in a row, we received notes like this.

One day, we were having lunch and talking about it.

"Mrs. O'Connell expects everything to be perfect," said Romaine. "I know we have to do well, but she carries it too far."

"That's right," said Beverly. "Those O'Connell's love their money and are filthy rich. We maids mean nothing to them. Any time one of us goes to the office, they look at us like dirt."

Everyone agreed. At the beginning of the summer, Mrs. O'Connell was a woman who hardly smiled. She was too formal in the way she dealt with all employees and was very cold in the way she related to all of them. I didn't want to get on her bad side; so I did the best I could in housekeeping. Besides, I already felt attracted to her for some reason. Previously, she had worked as a lawyer in Florida, and her hobby was skydiving. Because of this, the other employees respected and even admired her, but they never cared to be close friends with her. I, myself, had always felt attracted to the least likeable people. That had always been in my nature. I soon got into the habit of speaking to her every time I saw her, and she started to become more pleasant toward me.

One morning when we received our assigned rooms, I noticed that for over a week I had been assigned the main office and Mrs. O'Connell's room in the Old Inn.

"Mrs. O'Connell told me that she wants either you or Shirley to do those jobs," said Romaine.

"She likes me for some reason," I said. "Maybe it's because I'm in the Christian Ministry."

"It may be that," said Romaine.

I had been there for two weeks. It was at this time that David Mix, my co-worker in the Christian Ministry, arrived at Mt. Pisgah. I was visiting Janet, a Puerto Rican woman who had arrived a week after me and worked in the office. A red-haired man with a beard and glasses arrived outside the door.

"Excuse me," he said. "Do you know where I can find Sara Kemp?"

"I'm she," I said.

"I'm David Mix. I'll be working with you this summer."

Within an hour, I had shown Dave around, and we later had our first meeting in the main room of the Old Inn.

"I've talked with the ministry committee," I said. "They don't hold regular meetings, but they will meet if we ever need to. We are to give the offering money to Mrs. O'Connell to hold for us. They will pick it up every two weeks. We also have permission to hold the church services in the Old Inn Sunday mornings, and in the evenings we can have them at the campfire circle. I also mentioned to them that we'll be campground calling."

"Did you start the church services?"

"I started them last week."

"I was thinking of starting a Bible study. Would you have any problem with leading that?"

"Yes, I have been a Christian for only eighteen months and don't know much about the Bible."

"We can both work at it," said Dave.

When I had applied for a job with A Christian Ministry in the National Parks, I never expected to get the job. Well, imagine my surprise when I received a letter informing me about a job offer! When I accepted, I was assigned to one of the hardest areas. I learned this when I learned what the O'Connell's were like.

One day I ran into Janet on her way back to her cabin, and she was in tears.

"What's the matter?" I asked.

"Mrs. O'Connell said that I'm just not sharp enough for work in the office. I'm to start working in housekeeping tomorrow."

She had previously worked the pantry in the kitchen and had asked for a job in the office. She had only worked there for a few days.

"Do you want to talk?"

"Want to come back to my room with me? I don't want anyone to see that I'm crying."

As we talked, Janet said that she was thinking of quitting. I tried to encourage her to stay on by telling her that Romaine was not hard to work for and the housekeeping staff was not around the O'Connell's that much. Janet still decided to quit.

"Do you think I'm being unreasonable?" she asked me.

"No," I finally agreed. "No job is worth making yourself miserable over."

Why was I still there? Why hadn't I walked out by now? Already a bond was starting to develop between Mrs. O'Connell and me. She was pleasant toward me and always spoke to me. I liked her enough, but she would probably end up in the past like everyone I had known. She did not treat me as badly as the other maids, and she did send me to do odd jobs before sending the others. Romaine did tell me that she just wanted certain people to do certain things. Still, the other maids were just as good at their jobs. I still felt drawn to her. Why? Maybe it was because of my attraction to the least likeable people.

I was also developing other close relationships with the housekeeping staff. Cheryl, who had trained me on my first day, quit soon after my arrival. Irene quit in July when she developed back trouble. Meanwhile, Romaine hired two more maids. She had been after her and Gerald's daughter, Sherry, to work with us, and soon after Sherry, Romaine hired Brenda. Sherry's husband, Allen, later came to work with us as a maid and a handyman.

We soon started calling ourselves the Maid Brigade. Throughout the summer, we made dull housekeeping fun. If one of us had rooms in bad shape, she would still be working when the rest were done. That was when we would help her out. When we all got together in one room, there was no telling what would happen! Every day we would get into battles with cleaning fluids. Armed with bottles of Windex and GP Forward, we would go outside and chase each other up and down the balconies. If we weren't battling with cleaning fluids, we would be after each other with brooms and plungers. Romaine could never help laughing at us, and she sometimes joined us in our crazy antics. Knowing a whole repertoire of jokes, I would add to the fun by letting loose with some.

One day when we were all in one room, Shirley announced, "Hey, look what I found, three candy bars!"

"I get them. They're in my room," said Beverly.

"No, I found them. They're mine!"

The next minute four other maids were on top of Shirley, fighting for those candy bars. Brenda got them, and she wasn't giving them up. Romaine was laughing in the doorway.

"This is the craziest crew I ever saw! If any of the O'Connell's walks in some time, we're all fired!"

Well, Bruce did "walk in." Romaine told me about it afterwards. I had been working in the A building when she told me.

"We better be more careful when we horse around," she told me.

"Did somebody get caught?" I asked.

"Yeah, the others were horsing around. They were out riding brooms, and Bruce caught them. He said we can have some fun but no roughhousing around."

We were more discreet after that.

Not all of the times I had over the summer were fun. One evening Dave wanted to go on a hike. There was still plenty of daylight left, and we could be back before dark.

"Hey," I said after a while. "I wonder where this trail goes."

"Let's find out," said Dave.

It was a beautiful day. Everything was in full bloom. At certain places on the trail, we could get a good view of the Smokies.

"It's going to be dark soon. We better start back," I said eventually.

"Oh, let's go on. We'll find our way back."

Well, Dave was an Eagle Scout. He should have been able to find the way back at night.

We did start back an hour later, but it got too dark for us to see. We got on to a wrong trail and kept falling over logs and rocks.

"Are you okay?" I asked Dave when he had one bad fall.

"Oh, I don't know," he moaned.

Fortunately, he wasn't hurt badly. We decided to stay where we were until morning. So we stayed all night on a bed of rocks. Dave slept off and on all night. I couldn't sleep because I was afraid of never waking up again. I did a lot of thinking that night, about people who had gotten close to me over the summer, about the fun we had together in housekeeping, about how my family had never been close. I had been raised in a distant family, but I still thought about my family that night. Would I ever see those people again? I mostly thought about Mrs. O'Connell. She really did care about me. We had started to develop a deeper friendship. I would go to clean the main office every morning, and I would tell her jokes just to get her to smile and laugh. She had even started joking with me and smiling more lately. It gives me pleasure to make people laugh, and I had even more pleasure in making her laugh. At first, she had not been a happy person, and her first love was money. Because she was always trying to earn more money, she had made herself miserable. Would we end up staying in touch? Maybe, but maybe not. We had grown on each other like fungus. I would miss her, but staying in touch probably wouldn't last—or would it?

With thoughts like these, I waited out the night. Dave and I found our way back in the morning, but we both had to report to work later on.

"Let's go back to our rooms and not say anything to anyone," he told me. "We probably won't get much sympathy."

I got cleaned up and went to work.

The Maid Brigade knew that something was wrong.

"Why are you so quiet?" they kept asking me.

Romaine was just as concerned. She came to a room where I was working.

"Are you sick, Hon?" she asked as she made one of my beds.

"Why?"

"You act like you don't feel good. If you're sick, you let me know."

She sympathized with me. She took the time to help me clean my rooms.

"Take tomorrow off, and get better," she told me at the end of the day.

"Yesterday was my day off."

"That's all right. "I'm giving everybody two days off this week since we're not full."

I rested the next day, and my bed was never more comfortable! That afternoon I learned just how much Mrs. O'Connell cared about me. I went to the office to ask her for a forty-dollar advance since I was low on cash.

"Are you all right?" was the first thing she asked as she put her arm around me. No questions asked about why I couldn't make it to work.

"I will be."

"You will be? Is there anything I can do for you?"

"No thanks."

"Are you sure? I have aspirin, cough syrup, cold tablets…"

"I brought medicine with me."

"If there's anything I can do for you, let me know."

"Okay. Thanks for your concern."

"I am concerned about you!"

Well, it just so happened that Dave mentioned our adventure to another employee, and the next thing you know everyone knew about it! Of course word got around to the Maid Brigade who gave me the nickname Rocky Top. I went back to work the next day, and all I heard was "Good Old Rocky Top!"

Right after this, Mrs. O'Connell became even more of a friend, and we grew even closer for the rest of the summer. She really did care about me. A touch on the shoulder, the way she greeted me in the mornings, and the way she joked with me made this obvious.

Maybe she and the Maid Brigade would never be just a part of my past like other friends. Then again, maybe we would drift apart. We would probably never hear from each other again. Growing up in a distant family made it hard for me to stay in touch with friends that I always made. We had always drifted apart after some letters were written. That doesn't mean that I ever forgot about them. I loved them in my own way, but not enough to stay in touch. The hardest thing for me to say to anybody was "I love you."

"You'll have to write to us," Allen told me one day when we were on our lunch break. The summer was quickly ending.

"If I have the time," I said.

"You should be able to find the time," said Romaine.

"I have more than just my schoolwork," I said. "I'm involved in activities at school, and I tutor when I can."

Maybe that wasn't much of an excuse, but it was the only one I had. I didn't want to hurt them.

"Mrs. O'Connell sure has changed over the summer," I said to change the subject.

"Yes, she sure has," said Romaine. "It's a wonder to even see her smile."

Mrs. O'Connell really had changed over the summer. She seemed to be an entirely different person from the one I had known at the beginning of the summer. Anyone meeting her for the first time wouldn't believe that she had been such a cold person. I had asked her Labor Day off so that I could leave to start school on time.

"Then who would I have to giggle with?" she had asked.

One night Dave and I went out to play a few rounds of miniature golf. We only had another week to work before returning to school.

"One more week," I said. "You know, I'm going to miss Mrs. O'Connell. She has become the closest friend I have down here."

"She really cares about you," said Dave. "You're like a daughter to her."

I was pleasantly surprised.

"Do you really think so?"

"Well, she never had any daughters, and when you were sick, she checked on you."

She had been like a mother to me. Because of my childhood, I had never been close to my own parents. My father had worked night shifts as a tool and dye maker; so I didn't know him well as a child. Because of this, he had hardly been around to do a man's work at the house. We had never had much time to do things together as a family. A distance had grown among my brother, sister, parents, and myself over the years. As a result, I had found it difficult to put down roots anywhere. Maybe it would be different this time. Maybe I would stay in touch with Mrs. O'Connell and the Maid Brigade when I left. No, maybe not. We would probably drift apart. It had always been that way with others I had known.

I had just clocked out for the last time.

"I'll give you my address," said Romaine. "Write to us at least once."

I grabbed a paper, wrote down my address and phone number, and handed to Romaine. Would it last? Probably not.

That night I went to the main office to say goodbye to Mrs. O'Connell.

"Don't say goodbye, or I'll start to cry!" she said walking away from me.

"I want to talk to you."

She stopped and turned to face me.

"You have my address so you can send me my paycheck?"

"I have it at home."

Then she said, "I love you very much!"

"I love you too."

"Promise me you'll write?"

"Well…uh…yes, if I have time."

Sighing, she drew me to her in an embrace, and we held each other a moment.

Again she said, "Promise me you'll write?"

I finally weakened.

"Yes."

COMMUNITY NURSING

It was almost noon, time to be at my volunteer job at the hospital. I put out my cigarette, went through the double doors and up the steps. The elevators were on my right. Pressing the up button, I waited. It only took a few seconds for the doors to open. The elevator took me to the fourth floor. I reported to Millie, the receptionist and my supervisor. We greeted each other cheerfully.

"Hi Kathy. How are you doing?"

"Great! Our church choir practice is tonight."

"I started our practices last week. Here are some lab sheets to be alphabetized."

"I'll get right on it."

"Then there are some educational sheets to be pulled."

"No problem."

I sat at the volunteers' desk and began putting the papers into their proper order according to the patients' last names. They were computer printed; so there was no difficult handwriting to transcribe. After I had been working for about fifteen minutes, Millie brought over some more papers.

"Here are some more," she told me.

"No big deal."

These were some occupational and physical therapy sheets filled out by hand. I finished the lab sheets and began on the therapy sheets, sometimes asking Millie what the names were.

An hour later, I finished putting the papers in order.

"Thank you, and God bless," Millie told me.

"I guess you want them in the patients' slots in medical records?" I asked.

"Correct."

I took the papers to the medical records room where Karla and Sherry worked.

"Hi Kathy," they said together.

"Hi."

To Karla I said, "When are you having your hysterectomy?"

"A week from today; I'm a little scared."

"Just leave it in God's hands," I told her.

"I'm trying to, but it's not easy. I'm also having trouble concentrating on my work."

"We'll be praying for you," said Sherry.

"I appreciate that."

I pulled up a chair and began filling the papers into the slots with the letters on them. It only took a few minutes. The phones kept ringing nonstop. Millie, as well as the secretaries, would answer patiently and page different nurses.

I finished the filing and got a pile of checklists from a bin on Karla's desk. By referring to a current list of patients, I could find out which names were still active. These I stacked into a pile. The nonactive ones I filed into the patients' slots. Once that was done, I began referring to the checklists in the pile to pull educational sheets out of labeled slots. I noticed that some were low, and I made copies of those. A lot of times, there would be quite a few sheets for each patient. Just about every one needed a sheet for anticoagulant therapy. Quite a few were for diabetes. Even more needed sheets for special diets.

"Lots of these people are in said shape," I told Karla and Sherry.

"Yes, God love them," said Sherry who was emptying the charts of people who had been discharged.

"I hope when I get older, I won't have the problems these elderly people have," said Karla as she typed up labels for folders.

Sally, one of the secretaries, came and asked if we needed with anything.

"Yes," said Sherry. "If you could finish dumping these charts so I can work on the billing, that would be a great help."

"I'll be glad to."

Sherry went to her computer, while Sally took her place at the table. Several of the nurses came in during the next couple of hours to check their mail slots. One of them, named Betty, came in and offered to pull out some more checklists of new patients' needs, which she gave me to take care of. I had almost finished pulling the educational sheets I had gotten from Karla's desk, but there were only a few new ones.

"Would you mind if I go have my cigarette break?" I asked.

"No problem at all," said Karla.

I took the elevator downstairs and went outside. As I smoked, I thought of how blessed I was to work with such nice, Christian people. It was a nice change from other jobs I had had in which people constantly swore at each other or would come to work with a hangover. It was people in community nursing who made my job so much fun. I finished my smoke and went back upstairs.

"I'm back," I said, entering medical records.

"Have a nice smoke?" asked Sherry.

"Sure did."

Sally and Betty had left. I noticed Amy, another volunteer, filing some papers into patients' slots.

"Today's my last day," she said. "I'm leaving for college the day after tomorrow."

"Well, write to us and let us know how school is going," said Sherry.

"It's my first year, and I'm a little nervous," said Amy.

"You'll do fine," said Sherry as she finished making some printouts from the computer. "You're a smart girl."

"Well, pre-med is not an easy major."

"Just pray about it, and leave it in God's hands," said Karla after she had finished paging a nurse who had a phone call.

"That's just what we were telling you earlier," said Sherry.

"So practice what you preach," I told her jokingly as I started to sort the educational sheets into the four different nursing teams' piles.

"That's easier said than done," said Amy filing the last paper.

"That's how I felt before giving my life to the Lord," I said. "I started college being scared stiff. At the same time, I was renting from Eileen, a lady who's a Christian. I noticed she had something in her life that I lacked. She always seemed so happy, while I felt so empty inside."

"So, what did you do?" asked Amy.

"I asked her what she saw in religion that made her so happy, and she said that once you give your life to God, you just don't want to go back to your old ways. Well, I was struggling with a chemistry problem one night, and I got to think about how hard it was for me to deal with different things in life. Then I thought about how easy it was for Eileen to cope with everything because she has something special in her life. So, I decided, then and there, to give my life to God. I went to bed that night and woke up the next morning with the emptiness inside me completely gone."

"Awesome!" said Amy. "I am a Christian, but college is a big step. Yet, I will pray about it and get the strength I need from God."

"I'll remember that too," said Karla. "Just by leaving my surgery in God's hands will make it easier to deal with."

Amy got up to leave.

"It's been nice working with all of you," she said. "I'll be in touch. Thanks for sharing your story with us Kathy."

"You bet!"

I gathered up the educational sheets.

"I have to file these in the nursing bins."

"Okay, thanks for taking care of those," said Sherry.

"No problem. Good luck in school, Amy."

"Thanks."

Millie was manning the front desk, and the phones were still ringing nonstop. Several nurses and secretaries were rushing to different places in the office. Others were at their desks either doing paper work or answering phones.

"Get those teaching sheets done?" asked Millie.

"Yep, just have to file them at their places."

"Good job!"

I went around to the four nursing teams' stations, placing the papers into the bins.

"So you're the one who fills up our bins!" said Fred, a male nurse.

"Yep! I love making work for you," I joked.

He laughed.

"Do you have anything else for me to do?" I asked Millie.

"Yeah, I have several kinds of forms to be copied."

She handed me the originals.

"I need two hundred of these requests for nursing services on white paper, one hundred of these fax cover sheets on white paper, and one hundred fifty occupational therapy forms on pale yellow paper."

"I'll get right on it."

I turned on the copier, laid the first sheet on it, and pressed the start button.

"I hope this cooperates," I told Millie.

"Yeah, it can be cantankerous."

Papers did get jammed in the copier if it was used too much. I began to count the copies in Spanish as they came out of the machine. Nurses were still going in and out, and secretaries were still rushing around the office. It took about ten minutes to get all the copies made and put into their right places.

"These envelopes need return addresses stamped on them," said Millie.

"No problem at all," I said taking the box of envelopes and rubber stamp to the volunteers' desk.

I began pressing the rubber stamp to the ink box and stamping the envelopes. There were well over a hundred in the box. By the time I finished that job, an hour had gone by.

"I got them all stamped," I said to Millie.

"Wow! You're fast!"

"Is there anything else?"

"No, I think that's about it for the day. You're a great help! God bless you. Have fun at choir practice tonight."

"I will; I had fun today. Guess I'll see you next week."

"Yep. Thanks for everything. Again, God bless."

"God bless."

I walked past medical records.

"See you next week," I said to Sherry and Karla.

"See you," said Sherry.

"Thanks for everything," said Karla.

"That's what we're here for, to help each other as God's children," I said.

I went to catch the elevator to the first floor. It had been another day of being a blessing to others.

The Drop-In Center

Kathy turned the key in the lock, opening the door. She walked in, stomping snow from her boots and put the "Open" sign in the window. Turning on the lights, she made her way to the kitchen, laid the daily newspaper on the table, and started a pot of coffee. Going back to the foyer, she wrote her name on the sign-in sheet and the time she opened up. There were several messages on the answering machine for Karen, the executive director. These Kathy wrote down on the memo pad and left on her desk.

Going back to the kitchen, she unlocked the snack cupboard and got out a bag of chips, which she poured in a bowl and set on the table. Time to unload the dishwasher. As she was doing this, Leroy came in.

"Hi Sunshine," he said. "How are you today?"

"I'm okay. How are you?"

"Good," he said leaning his cane against the wall. "How would you like some macaroni and cheese with hamburger for lunch?"

"Sounds good to me," said Kathy as she put away the last of the dishes.

"Great! I'll go over to the store for the stuff and start cooking around noon."

Kathy put fifty cents in the soda machine and pressed the Pepsi button. Leroy sat at the table and began reading the paper.

"I see that the First Commonwealth Bank got robbed yesterday," he said.

"Any one get hurt?"

"No, but the police are still looking into it."

Jim, Karen's assistant, came in the back door.

"Good morning," he said as he put a gallon of iced tea in the fridge. "Any messages on the answering machine?"

"A few for Karen," said Kathy, sipping her soda.

"There have been people talking on the phone too long," said Jim. "Kathy, could you please print out some notices about the five minutes allowed except for emergencies?"

"I'll do it right now."

She got up and went to the computer room. Jim joined Leroy at the table.

"Any good news in the paper?" he asked.

"There never is. If you want to get depressed, look at the paper."

"Not too many people have been depressed lately. There haven't been any calls to the suicide hot line."

"No," said Leroy. "Just a lot of gossip."

Bob came in, complaining about the snow that needed to be shoveled in the parking lot.

"I spend more time working outside than I do in here!" he said.

"Have a cup of coffee before you start," Jim said.

Bob poured a cup and added some cream and sugar.

"Some day, I'm going to go to work as a paramedic and get off disability," he said, as he stirred his coffee.

"If you get a good job in this town, you can count your blessings," Leroy said.

"Getting a good job at the hospital will be my best bet," said Bob.

"Well, I'm a retired chef," said Leroy. "I can just sit back and enjoy life."

"I'm only in my forties," said Jim. "I still have a long way to go 'till retirement."

"I just turned twenty-six and am still young enough to get a good job," said Bob.

Kathy came back in and tacked a notice on the bulletin board near the phone.

"I taped notices in the foyer and in the TV room," she said.

"Thanks a lot," Jim said. "I just wish we could pay you volunteers for all the work you do."

"I'd love to go back to work and get off disability," said Kathy. "But who would hire me at my age?"

"You're still young," said Leroy. "And only in your forties."

"Yeah, but not too many people would hire someone my age in this town because being in your forties is considered old."

"Guess I'll go shovel snow and salt the porches and sidewalks," said Bob as he finished the last of his coffee.

"Have fun!" joked Leroy.

Bob put on his coat, got the shovel from the closet and went out back. Karen and Anna, the center's treasurer, came in right after he went out.

"Hi," said Anna.

"Hi guys! What's up?" Karen said cheerfully.

"My age," said Kathy.

"The sky," said Leroy.

"You guys kill me!" said Karen laughing.

"There are some messages on your desk," said Jim.

"Okay, thanks," she said going to the office she shared with him.

"Kathy," said Anna, pouring some iced tea. "Would you like another cat? Our kids brought home a stray."

"No, two are enough for Rob and me, but just out of curiosity, what kind of cat is it?"

"It's a beautiful long-haired white male with green eyes. He's really very sweet, but he eats like a horse."

"Pets aren't allowed where I live," said Leroy.

"My roommate has allergies," said Jim.

"We might end up keeping him," said Anna. "People are looking for kittens, and our kids really love him."

"How does he get along with your other two cats?" asked Kathy.

"Well, he gets along with Cali, our female, but Blackey, our male, is very jealous."

"Keep them in separate rooms and introduce them slowly. You can also put things with each cat's scent on them in their rooms. That way, they can get used to each other."

"Is that what you did with your cats?"

"No. Echo and Shiane are from the same litter. They get along great!"

"What's this about cats?" asked Willow, the center's president, stamping snow from her boots.

"We were just talking about our personal cat problems," said Anna.

"My husband would kill me if I brought home a cat," said Willow nibbling on some chips.

"Rob and I wouldn't know what to do without our cats," said Kathy.

"Well, if we keep this cat, we're not getting any more pets," said Anna.

"Anna, did we get that check yet from United Way?" asked Willow.

"It came in the mail yesterday."

"Let's get to the bank and put it in."

"Let's go up to our office and get it now."

Anna and Willow went upstairs.

"Guess I'll go help Karen schedule some group therapy for this week. Talk to you guys later," said Jim leaving the kitchen.

"Guess we can watch TV until it's time to start lunch," said Leroy.

"Maybe I can get in some typing and computer lessons today," said Kathy. "That doesn't seem likely though."

"Yeah, the people in this town don't know how handy it is to type and know about computers to get a job."

Kathy and Leroy went to the TV room.

All day, people came and left. Some guys went to the basement for a poole tournament, which was supervised by Jim. The first prize was two dollars, and the second prize was one dollar. Delores and Mack, two more volunteers, came in and led an anger management group, which lasted for an hour. This was a group that was very popular because of the anger problems that most of the consumers faced. They all had had rough lives because of different kinds of abuse in their childhoods and even from relationships as adults. Max, a counselor at the mental health clinic, came in for an hour and led a support group for those with drug and alcohol problems. Karen and Jim provided some crafts for anyone wanting to do some projects. Leroy walked to the grocery store to get the food for lunch. He even bought some Kool-Aid. He gave Karen the receipt, and she wrote him a reimbursement check. While he was fixing lunch, Kathy gave a typing and computer lesson to Gwen, a consumer hoping to go back to work.

At about a quarter to one, Leroy had lunch ready. Karen, Jim, Anna, and Willow joined everyone else in the kitchen as Leroy mixed up some Kool-Aid.

"When you're done, please rinse off your dishes and put them in the dishwasher," he said.

"Very good," said Bob relishing every bite. "Sure is worth a hard day of work."

"We appreciate you," said Karen.

"We appreciate all of our volunteers," said Willow.

"This sure is a nice place to come to just to get out of the house," said Gwen.

"I used to sit around all day feeling depressed until I heard about this place from the mental health clinic," said Kathy. "Never thought I'd meet the man of my dreams here."

"How long have you and Rob been married?" asked Roger, another volunteer and consumer.

"It will be thirteen years June twentieth."

"Where has Rob been keeping himself?" asked Anna. "I haven't seen him in a while."

"He's content just to stay home these days. He loves to listen to the TV evangelists and read the Bible. I'm usually content to stay home with him, but I like to go out and work at both of my volunteer jobs."

"How do you like your other job at the hospital?" asked Leroy.

"Oh, I love it!"

"Do you work with the patients?" asked Roger.

"No, I work as a clerical assistant in Community Nursing. The best part is that I don't answer the phones."

"I still do volunteer work at my church," said Gwen.

"What all do you do there?" asked Karen.

"Type up Sunday bulletins and help with the newsletters. It's a lot of fun."

Just then, Rob came in.

"Help yourself to some lunch," said Leroy.

"Thank you," said Rob putting some food on a plate and pouring a cup of coffee.

"Just thought I'd get out of the house for a while."

"Good to see you," said Kathy kissing him.

"Good to see you Honey."

"Hey! No kissing allowed here!" joked Roger.

"That wasn't kissing," said Kathy. "That was lunch."

Everyone chuckled.

"It's good to joke around," said Karen. "Or things will get to you."

"It's especially good if you have an anger problem," said Rob.

"Yeah, or you'll only get sicker," said Roger. "I once read that laughter is the best medicine. "I've seen people on TV being cured from cancer just by laughing hard," said Kathy.

"Well, my wife taught me how too laugh," said Rob. "So I should live a long time."

"These days people don't live long because of drinking, drugs, and smoking," said Leroy.

"If they get help here, they can get over it," aid Gwen. "I've never done those things, but I hear it's hard to quit."

"You're smart," said Roger. "I had one heck of a time giving up drinking. So don't even start."

"I have asthma, and I smoke," said Karen. "I'd love to quit."

"I quit for a couple of years and started again," said Anna.

"I've quit cold turkey a couple of times and always started up again," said Kathy. "Now I really don't want to quit."

"Never have smoked and never will either," said Rob.

"There's plenty left if anyone wants more," said Leroy.

"No more for me," said several people.

Nobody got up to get any more; so Leroy began putting leftovers in the fridge. Every one rinsed off the dishes and put them in the dishwasher. Leroy put in the powdered soap, pressed the buttons for the right settings and started it up. Karen and Anna wiped the countertops, table, and stove.

"Might as well get back to work," said Willow putting the Kool-Aid in the fridge, and leaving the kitchen.

She and Anna went back upstairs, and Jim and Karen went back to their office. Some of the consumers and volunteers went back to their different activities, and others signed out and left for the day.

"Well, it's about two o'clock," said Kathy to Rob. "Guess my work here is done for the day."

"Ready to go?"

"Ready when you are."

As Rob and Kathy were getting their coats, they passed by Karen and Jim's office.

"You guys leaving us?" asked Karen.

"Yep," said Kathy. "See you next week."

"Thanks for all your help," said Jim.

"You bet! Have a good week."

"Kathy," said Karen. "Would you like to start a newsletter for the center?"

"Sure, I have a bachelor's in compository writing."

"Do you think you can write an article about mental illness and even get therapists and doctors at the clinic to write articles as well? You can bring them in next week and use one of our computers to put it together."

"Yeah, that sounds like fun!"

"You'd be good at that, Hon," said Rob. "You're very creative."

"Great!" said Karen. "See you next week."

"See you," said Rob and Kathy going out the front door.

"We have some good people that come here," said Jim. "I really like my job."

"Yeah," said Karen. "The people at the clinic and the ones that come here are just as good as any one else."

A Need For Solace

Zombies everywhere as I walk through the halls. I'm here for the same reason they are. We sit on the back porch smoking cigarettes or in the dull-colored rooms watching TV. Later we drift into the dining room and eat but taste nothing. We will all leave someday—one after another. Some of us will leave with little strangers. Others will leave by themselves. Can we avoid the same mistake again? Can we find good jobs and be accepted in society again? Can they finish high school and go on to college? Having finished college, will I find a good job? What will become of the stranger inside me?

Like the others, I messed around. Two men I slept with. Can I live a cleaner life? Perhaps for a while. Then it will be different boyfriends—each one on different evenings. Yes, I will play around again as I had learned to as a child.

THE WAIT

How long has it been? Two months? No, three months. The last time he had been there was the week before Thanksgiving. Why hasn't he been back? She had called and told him that she missed him.

Careful not to get up too fast, she got out of bed and went to the kitchen to get her breakfast—a bowl of cereal, a glass of orange juice, and some fruit. That would be good for her condition. She wouldn't be working until afterwards. Another month until the time came.

She made her bed and got dressed for the day. Had to get to the store today. She walked down the dark hallway, past the closed doors, and past the broken window.

Then she passed the dilapidated houses on her street, the group of kids with worn-out jeans and holey T-shirts. Occasionally making eye contact with people before they looked away. She bought what she needed—milk, fruit, cereal, and lunchmeat. Back to the red shingled building badly in need of repair. Why not call him again? No, if he cared, he would be there.

She lay in bed and read for an hour. A walk around the block. The Young and the Restless at 12:30. A sandwich, glass of milk, and an apple for lunch. Her doctor's appointment was at 2:00. She walked the five blocks to the clinic where she registered at the receptionist's desk by writing her name and the numbers of her blue medical card. Then she only had to wait for a few minutes. The nurse weighed her, did a urinalysis, and took her blood pressure. The doctor measured her belly and listened to the heartbeat, saying that everything was going fine. Her next appointment would be next week.

Back at her apartment where she heard a knock at the door and felt excitement. She opened the door to the landlord who had come for the rent. She wrote out a check for him. The evening she spent in front of the TV, holding her belly and feeling the movement inside.

Mornings, she woke up to have breakfast or lie in bed to watch TV. Before it got too hot in the day, she would go run errands or take walks. She spent some afternoons napping or reading, but always listening for the knock at the door.

"You could go into labor next week," the doctor told her the next week.

"What's today's date?"

"Today's July first."

She decided to admit herself to the home for unwed mothers. There she fell into the routine of getting up in the mornings for breakfast. Then she would spend the rest of the morning reading in the sunroom. Lunch was at 12:00. Afternoons watching TV or taking walks on the grounds. Supper was at 6:00. Some evening residents went to movies. They were all younger than she was and had no idea what parenting was like. They would talk about how much fun they would have with their babies.

How can I manage? she thought. If he's not coming back, she would consider adoption. She finished the book she was reading and borrowed more from the library.

Mona, a staff member, offered to take the residents to a concert. She went just to speed up the wait. All that day she felt slight pains in her back. The next day she had a doctor's appointment. A woman doctor examined her and told her that it could happen any day now. That night Mona offered to take them to the store, and she went along just to browse.

A pain in her lower back woke her at ten till six the next morning. For an hour, she lay there feeling the pains every fifteen minutes. Getting up she got dressed and went to get the staff member on duty who took her to the hospital. She was admitted and later lay on a bed listening to the baby's heartbeat on the monitor and feeling the pains increasing and getting closer together. The nurses came in regularly to check on her. A medical student gave her ice chips.

"Well," said the lady doctor she had seen the day before. "I see you went into labor the next day."

"I didn't think it would be this soon."

"They sometimes decide to come early."

"When is your baby due?"

"It's due next month."

"Is this your first?"

"Yes," the doctor said.

"Mine too, but I hope not to go through this again."

"This is the worst pain to go through, but it's quickly forgotten."

The afternoon dragged on as she tried to concentrate on the TV programs. They finally decided that it was late enough in labor to give her something for the pain. She was aware of the IV needle being poked into her arm. Almost immediately she felt dizzy, then drowsy. Drifting in and out of consciousness, she was barely aware of the fetal heartbeat and people going in and out. All at once she woke up feeling the urge to push.

"Put your legs back and push," said the lady nurse. "That's it. Beautiful! Another contraction? Give another push. Very good! We're going to wheel you into delivery now."

She felt herself moved onto the gurney. Through the pain, she was barely aware of activity around her as they wheeled her out. Moved onto a table and feet placed in the stirrups.

"That's it. Push!" said the male doctor.

She pushed determined to end the pain.

"Give just a little push."

She pushed slightly. Then a baby's cry.

"It's a girl."

WHO'S NEXT?

"I'll be back tonight."

"I won't be home tonight," she lied.

"When?"

"I'll call you."

She closed the door behind him and went to the bathroom where she flushed the rubber down the toilet. Must get more for Bill tonight. She stopped at the drugstore on her way to work. There she went through the motions of waiting on customers and answering the phone. Home for a quick supper. Then Bill's arrival.

"You bring out the man in me!" he said undressing her. "Your body is mine."

Mechanically he loved her.

"I better be going," he said a couple hours later.

"You can't spend the night?"

"Gotta get home to my wife."

She was off the next day. She cleaned her apartment and did her laundry. In the afternoon she went to the grocery store. She picked out what she needed—half a gallon of milk, a loaf of bread, and a pound of cheese.

"Excuse me," said a man as she came outside. "Where can I find a pay phone?"

"There's one on the corner, but it eats up your money if you don't get an answer. The one on the other side of the parking lot works better."

"Thanks."

She started home and passed a mother pushing a stroller and felt a stab of envy. She had a man always there for her, always sharing her hopes and dreams. At night, emotionally and physically loving her. Discussing problems and sharing joys and sorrows. She wondered who she would see tonight. Maybe she would call David the way she said she would. She knew he would spend the night. Others, like Bill and Mike, would only come for an hour or so. Going to a pay phone, she placed a quarter in the slot and dialed his number. No answer.

"Need a ride?' called a voice as she came out of the booth.

It was the man she saw at the store. She noticed how distinguished he looked with his gray hair and the muscles on his arms.

"Sure, why not?"

"I've seen you around," he said as she got into his truck beside him. "Seems we should get to know each other."

"You from around here?" she asked him.

"Originally, but I've lived all over. What do you do?"

She liked the smell of his after-shave.

"I'm a travel agent."

"Work in a lot of places?'

"I've worked in several states. Meet a lot of interesting people that way."

She moved closer to him becoming more aware of the smell of his after-shave.

*   *   *

She moved closer to his sleeping body and looked toward the window seeing the first rays of sunlight starting to come in. He would be back. They all did. I'm a female Don Juan, she thought moving closer to him. She remembered being about ten or eleven and how those two men had told her she should know how to love. She remembered them going inside her. How scary it was; yet exciting!

"Don't tell anyone about this, or something bad will happen," they had told her. "Come back, or we'll find you."

She had gone back a lot over the next months. It ended when they moved away. She had grown to love the attention by that time and missed it. By the time she was in the eighth grade, she was doing a lot of flirting with guys and was dating a lot. He stirred next to her.

"Mornin'," he said. "You were beautiful last night."

"You weren't so bad yourself."

"You gotta work?"

"In a few hours."

"I better be going then."

She watched as he gathered his clothes up off the floor.

"Guess I'll be seeing you around," he said.

"Can I have your number?"

He wrote it for her on a slip of paper.

"I'll call you next week."

She wondered who it would be tonight.

Humanity

So I have a higher intellect and don't think like most people. Complex things come easily to me; while simple things are difficult for me. A lot of times I wonder about philosophical things and wonder about the purpose of life. Yet, I have personal feelings and have my favorite foods. Like many people, I watch my favorite TV programs and have my favorite clothes to wear. Over the years, I have listened to my favorite soft music and love God very deeply. Yes, I am human; yet long for love and a family.

MY CHOICE

Why am I on this college retreat? I am seeking some answers. Michael and I have one thing in common—we are lowly servants chosen by God. I love Michael, and I also love Jack. I hate being torn between the two. I am chosen by God and can not keep doing the things that I have been doing. A lot of times I can not bear the thoughts about the personal struggles and temptations that I face now. I have tried what I can to resolve this and am left with no other alternative except to break it off with Jack for his wife and family's sake. I have to do it, and it may cost me my apartment.

CHANGES

She gazed at the beautiful scenery of Shenandoah National Park, the place where she had worked last year. I don't want to be back here, she thought and went to the office to find out what her job would be. Kenny, the residency manager, told her that she would work as a cashier in the gift shop. He took her to meet the other two cashiers and show her around. Dottie and Mary, two older ladies, made her feel welcome as they showed her around the shop. They were both young at heart and fun loving. As she met other employees, she learned that there was a family like atmosphere to the place. Just like the wayside last year.

Might as well go back to my room and get settled in, she thought. She started unpacking. This was the fourth move she had made in one year—and also the hardest. She could just feel his body against her now. Such a gentle lover. He also loved and understood her as no other person did. He didn't try to stop her as she made arrangements to come to her next job in the national parks. Fool that she was to come. She would never find another one like him.

The rain was beating gently on her window. She slowly unpacked and arranged her knick-knacks on the shelf and dresser. Jars of food she also arranged on the shelf. Next to these she placed two seashells that Dave had given her at Myrtle Beach and an artificial flower in a crystal vase that she had bought at Mt. Pisgah National Park. A small glass statue of a praying child, a small olive wood communion cup, and a small plastic set of praying hand she placed on the end of the shelf. Her wooden cross she hung on the wall. Her letters about this job she placed in a box that she used as a filing cabinet.

All settled in until moving to her next position in the national parks. No, she would finish this contract and go back to Pennsylvania. Establish roots for herself. She would drop him a line and let him that she would be back.

*   *   *

No family life as a child and no roots anywhere. Then she met Joel. She had thought that it would like her other romances, and she would move on. However this was different. She had never loved a man as much as she loved Joel. This is my last position, she thought. Would they feel the same when she went back? Or will I get over him? Will he forget me and find someone else? If we get over each other, will I live the rest of my life like this? Will I always be on the move—always running from my childhood pain?

TOGETHER

We can't be together now, but we are still close at heart. Our love is stronger than friendship and binds us together for life. Alone I was before we met knowing part of me was missing. Distance does not separate us although my work took me far away. You are with me wherever I go. When I'm discouraged, I can hear you telling me to go on. You taught me how to enjoy life and live it while I can. Every day I pray that we can someday become one and be together for life.

CAN I DO IT?

He tells me that I'll make a good mother but I look at the scars on my body and wonder. He holds me and tells me what a good and gentle lover I am. The physical wounds have healed long ago, but I still feel the old childhood anger. It sometimes escapes when someone offends me. I look at the bulge in my middle and cry as a tear falls to my diamond as I remember how I agreed to have a baby. He will be home any minute, and we'll be going to his parents' place for dinner. To them, it is a celebration, but is it really?

A New Beginning

"Okay, you all did fine."

Attorney Brown announced the end of the oral final in Media Law. With a sense of relief, I went out to walk around the campus before catching the bus in an hour.

A girl was walking across campus in her stocking feet. Once more I saw students with hair dyed different colors, dressed in funky clothes. I passed through the library where students were cramming for finals and preparing term papers at the last minute. Again, I saw myself complaining with friends about the work in some classes, studying for exams and preparing term papers, making changes as I typed.

I passed the Engineering and Science building and again saw myself as a freshman in biology and chemistry classes. Again, I saw myself working the summers saving enough to pay for school.

I saw a job hunt, a struggle to be an established writer and loans to be paid back.

I walked up to Biddle Hall to catch the bus. As I stood there, I glanced back and saw the security guard locking the door.

ABOUT THE AUTHOR

Rocky T. Kinsley is the pseudonym of an author who focuses on the dark side of human nature and bases her writing in tihs book on personal experiences, especially with struggles in drug and alcohol abuse and mental illness. She is a graduate of the University of Pittsburgh in Johnstown, Pa. with a B. A. in writing and has had poems published by The International Library of Poetry. She lives in Seward, Pa. with her husband.